# THIS LITTLE PIG STAYED HOME

Written by Donna Guthrie
Illustrated by Katy Keck Arnsteen

Storybook Special™

**PRICE/STERN/SLOAN**
*Publishers, Inc., Los Angeles*
**1987**

*Dedicated to Liz Bevington*

Library of Congress Cataloging-in-Publication Data

Guthrie, Donna.
  This little pig stayed home.

  Summary: With an ulterior motive in mind, B. B. Wolf talks his way into the Pig home by offering to cook their dinner, but he modifies his plan when Aunt Delilah Pig offers him a job as chef in her health food restaurant.
  [1. Pigs—Fiction. 2. Wolves—Fiction]
I. Arnsteen, Katy Keck, ill.    II. Title.
PZ7.G9834Th  1987                    [E]              86-25367
ISBN 0-8431-1820-2

This little pig went to market,
This little pig stayed home,
This little pig had roast beef,
This little pig had none,
And this little pig cried "Boo Hoo! Boo Hoo!"
all the way home!

Mother Pig went to market while Penny Pig stayed home. Penny reached for her mother's big blue cookbook. She was going to make dinner for the family.

"What shall I fix for supper?" said Penny, turning the pages. "Pot roast? Father likes that. He's always saying, 'This little pig had roast beef.'" She flipped the pages to the section on vegetables. "But Aunt Delilah is coming and she's a vegetarian. If I serve roast beef, she will have none of it."

"Penny, Penny!" called her little brother. "Will you bring me some tea? Achoo!" Poor Winston was sick with a cold. He left school in the middle of French class and cried all the way home.

As Penny put on her apron, there was a knock at the door. It was B.B. Wolf. "Could you tell me," asked the wolf, "is this where the three little pigs live?"

"No," said Penny. "The three little pigs live two blocks over on Swine Crest."

B.B. placed a large, furry foot inside the door. "I see you're planning supper. What are you making?"

"I haven't decided yet," said Penny, trying to close the door.

"Perhaps I could help," said the wolf sweetly. "I have a secret recipe that's been in my family for years. I could make it for tonight's dinner."

"Is it good?" asked Penny.

"It's wonderful!" said B.B. It's called '*rôti du porc aux légumes*'. '*Aux légumes*' is French for 'with vegetables'. It's made with onions, turnips, okra and a special ingredient that I add at the very last moment."

"I don't know if my family likes French food," said the little pig.

"Trust me," said the wolf as he pushed Penny aside.

"I'll take care of everything. This will be the best supper that has ever been eaten!"

"Put a kettle of water on to heat," ordered the wolf. And Penny, not wanting to be contrary, put a large, filled pot on top of the stove.

"I'll need a large knife," said the wolf as he put on a chef's apron and hat.

"Why do you need a knife?" asked the little pig nervously.

"I need a knife to chop the vegetables, of course," he replied. The wolf was an expert with a knife. He chopped the turnips, parsley, onions and okra into tiny little pieces.

"Maybe I could finish the recipe for you," suggested Penny. "Just tell me the secret ingredient and you can be on your way."

"Oh, I couldn't do that," said the wolf, dropping the vegetables into the boiling water. "If I told you the last ingredient it wouldn't be a secret. I want tonight's meal to be a surprise for everyone."

Penny looked at the clock. "I'd better hurry and set the table. Mother, Father and Aunt Delilah will be here soon."

"Good idea," said the wolf, stirring the pot. "When they get here, my *rôti du porc* will be complete."
Winston heard voices in the kitchen. "Who is Penny talking to and what is '*rôti du porc*'?" he wondered. "I'll look it up in my French book. I hate surprises."
Winston turned to the page about food. "In English '*rôti du porc*' means . . .ROAST PORK! I'm pork and so are Penny, Mother, Father and Aunt Delilah. The stranger in the kitchen is planning to have us for his dinner!"

Winston took his French book and quietly crawled into the kitchen and under the table. "Pssst, Penny," whispered Winston. "Under here!"

"What are you doing out of bed?" demanded
Penny.
Winston pointed to "*rôti du porc*" in his French
book. Penny read the English words beside it and
her eyes grew wide with fright.

"Your family will be here soon," said B.B., smacking his lips.
"I think I can begin to add the final ingredient. Would you like to taste it before I do?"
Penny swallowed a spoonful of broth. "It's perfect," she said, "I wouldn't add a thing."
"Really?" said the wolf, taking a taste. "You're right, it *is* good. But I *always* add the last special ingredient."

In rushed Aunt Delilah carrying a long loaf of French bread.

"What is that delicious smell?" she asked. "I must have a taste."

"It isn't finished yet," said the wolf. "I must add one more thing to make it perfect."

Aunt Delilah dipped a spoon into the boiling broth. "Don't touch it! It is perfect! I will buy this recipe for my health food restaurant. What do you call it?"
"Well. . ." said the wolf slowly. "It's called. . ."

Just then Mother and Father came in. "I'm hungry—what's for dinner?" asked Father. He stopped and stared at the wolf in chef's clothing. "And who's this?"

"Not now," said Aunt Delilah, "I'm interviewing my new chef. He's about to tell me the last ingredient for this wonderful dish."

The wolf looked at Aunt Delilah and the other pigs. He thought of becoming a famous chef, giving cooking lessons, perhaps having a TV show of his own. Then, slowly, his hand moved over to the counter where the butcher knife lay. Penny and Winston gasped.

The wolf picked up. . .the pepper! "The last, most important ingredient is pepper!" he said, adding a pinch to the pot.

"There! It's finished. I call it *'rôti du porc aux légumes sans le porc'*!"

"You're hired," said Aunt Delilah. "Report tomorrow and bring this recipe with you."

"Good," said Father, "that's over. Let's eat."

And so the five little pigs and B.B. Wolf sat down to a wonderful meal of *rôti du porc aux légumes sans le porc*. . . or, in simpler terms, vegetable soup.